DISNEY'S
FAIRY TALE
THEATER

PRESENTS

*Mickey
and Minnie*

IN

Rapunzel

Adapted by Liane B. Onish

Illustrated by Len Smith & Adam Devaney

A **GOLDEN BOOK** • **NEW YORK**

Golden Books Publishing Company, Inc., New York, New York 10106

Once upon a time, in a faraway land, a husband and wife were expecting a baby.

One day the wife was looking out the window into the garden next door. She saw some lettuce, which was called rapunzel, growing there. Suddenly she had a great desire to eat some.

"My dear husband," she said, "I must have some rapunzel lettuce from that garden."

"That garden belongs to a witch," whispered the husband. "She is said to be the most fearsome witch in all the land. But if you want some rapunzel, then I will get it for you."

The husband knew he would have to find his way into the garden without being seen.

So late that night, the husband climbed
over the wall into the witch's garden.
Quickly, he picked some lettuce and was
about to leave, when . . .

"Who dares to steal lettuce from my beautiful garden?" an angry voice demanded.

"M-m-madame," the man stammered, staring at the witch, who had suddenly appeared. "My wife is expecting a baby, and she craves this rapunzel lettuce."

"I will let you have some of *my* lettuce, which *I* planted and which *I* have tended with such care," the witch replied. "But I want something in return. When the child is born you will give it to me!"

The unhappy man nodded his head in agreement and scrambled over the wall.

A few months later a beautiful baby girl was born
to the couple.

"What shall we name her?" asked the father as he
admired his new daughter.

Suddenly the witch appeared. "Her name will be Rapunzel, and she is mine! Remember your promise," she said to the father.

Then the witch took the child from the frightened parents and disappeared.

As the years passed, Rapunzel grew to be a beautiful young woman. She had soft skin and very long, thick hair, which she wore in a braid.

The witch was afraid someone would take Rapunzel from her, so she locked her in a high tower with no door and one window. The only way into the tower was through the window.

When the witch wanted to visit Rapunzel, she would stand at the bottom of the tower and call, "Rapunzel, Rapunzel, let down your hair."

Rapunzel would hang her long braid out the window and the witch would climb it.

Rapunzel would sit for hours at the window, watching the birds in the treetops and singing in her sweet, high voice.

One day, while Rapunzel was singing at the window, a handsome prince happened to ride by.

The prince rode closer and saw Rapunzel at the window. He wanted to talk with her but, even though he rode around and around the tower, he couldn't find a way in.

The prince rode home, puzzled. But he couldn't stop thinking about the lovely young woman he'd seen. He went back time and time again to watch her from a hiding place in the forest.

Then, one night, he saw the witch come and call to Rapunzel. He watched in amazement as the old woman climbed the long, golden braid. He stayed hidden until he saw her climb down again. He had decided what he would do.

The next day the prince came back to the tower. "Rapunzel, Rapunzel, let down your hair!" he called up to the window.

Rapunzel's long braid came tumbling toward the ground. The prince climbed up the braid and into the tower room.

At first Rapunzel was frightened. But the prince assured her that he was a friend.

The two spent long hours talking and laughing. Very soon they had fallen in love.

Suddenly they heard from below, "Rapunzel, Rapunzel,
let down your hair!" The witch had returned!
"She must not find you here!" Rapunzel cried.
But there was no place to hide in the little room.

Rapunzel had no choice but to let the witch climb up her braid. And when the old woman found the prince in the tower she flew into a rage.

"You'll not visit my Rapunzel again," she shrieked. With that she took up the heavy braid and cut it off.

"Now, go!" she shouted at the prince, and with a mighty shove, she pushed him out the window.

"No! Please!" cried Rapunzel as the prince fell. She ran to the window and leaned out so far that she, too, tumbled through it.

To the couple's good fortune, some flowering bushes grew thickly at the base of the tower. Their fall was cushioned by branches and leaves.

The prince lifted Rapunzel onto his horse, which was tethered nearby. Then the two rode off toward the prince's castle.

Soon Rapunzel was sharing a joyous reunion with her dear parents. The couple had yearned for their lost daughter during all the years she had been with the witch.

Not long after that, there was great happiness and celebration throughout the land when Rapunzel and the prince were married.

Rapunzel planted a beautiful garden near the castle, where she grew lots of the delicious lettuce that had given her her name.

The witch lived out her life locked up in the tower.

Of course, Rapunzel and her prince lived happily ever after.